PAW PATROL™

Pups Save the Party

PaRragon

Bath · New York · Cologne · Melbourne · Delhi
Hong Kong · Shenzhen · Singapore

One windy afternoon, the pups are in Katie's Pet Parlour, preparing a surprise birthday party for Chase.

"Streamers away!" says Rocky.

"Next up – the birthday cake!" says Katie.

"But who is keeping Chase busy and making sure he doesn't find out?" says Skye.

"Marshall is," says Rubble. "He can keep a secret... can't he?"

Marshall and Chase are at the park.

"It's too windy," calls Chase. "Maybe we should go and find the others."

"No! I mean, uh... it's nice here," says Marshall. "It's not like there's a big secret I have to keep..."

Suddenly, the wind gets so strong, it blows the pups onto the swings... and into a heap on the floor.

Back at the pet parlour, everyone is still busy getting ready for the party, when the lights go off.

"All the lights on the street are out, too," calls Rocky. "What happened?"

Ryder looks at his PupPad. "If the power is out, something must be wrong with one of the windmill turbines on Jake's Mountain."

"We won't have any music without electricity!" cries Skye.

"Or lights," says Rubble. "Maybe we can't have a party for Chase after all."

"No way!" says Ryder. He grabs his PupPad:
"PAW Patrol to the Lookout!"

The pups all race to the Tower, but there's no
electricity, so the lift isn't working!

"Marshall," says Ryder. "I need to use your ladder to get up there."

Marshall raises his ladder and Ryder climbs up into the Lookout.

He looks through the periscope. "A windmill blade broke," he says. "That's why there's no power."

"Pups, we have an emergency!" says Ryder. "Rocky, I need you to find something in your truck to fix that blade," he says.

"Marshall, we need your ladder to climb up it."

"Chase, the traffic lights will be out too – we need your siren and megaphone to direct traffic."

"And Skye, Rubble and Zuma," he whispers, "you look after the party!" The pups nod back.

"Let's do this!" bark the PAW Patrol.

Skye, Rubble and Zuma stay behind at the Lookout.

"Time to save Chase's party!" says Skye.

"What are we going to do?" asks Zuma.

"We'll have a party in the dark!" says Rubble.

"Yeah! We'll give Chase the best surprise party in the dark, ever!" barks Skye.

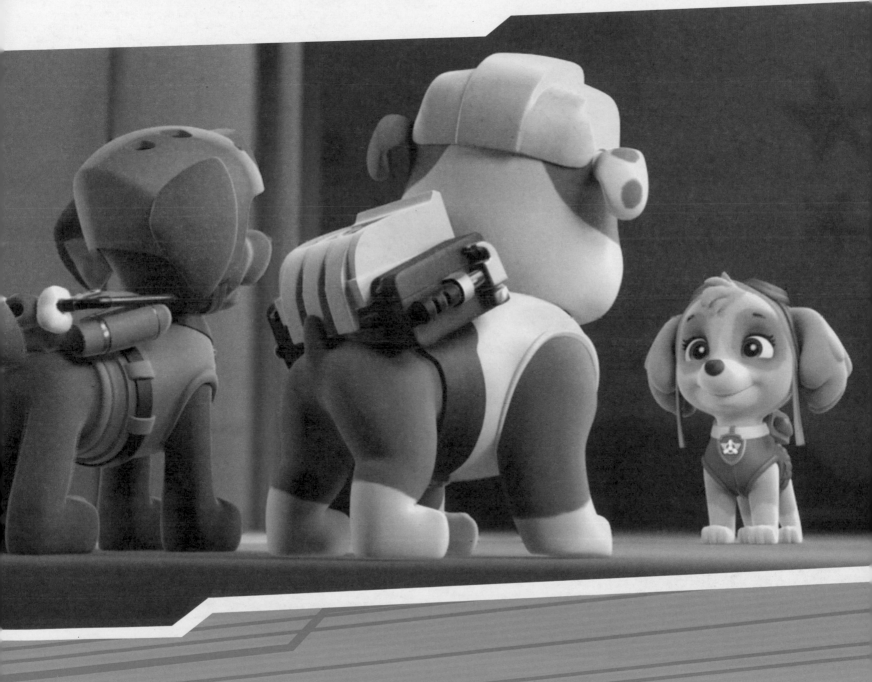

Over on Main Street, the traffic lights aren't working. There's a big traffic jam.

"We can't even cross the street," says Mayor Goodway. "And it's getting dark."

Chase arrives and gets straight to work with his megaphone.

"WOOF!" he barks. "Everyone going this way, go NOW! All the cars going that way, STOP!"

The drivers do as they're told and the traffic clears. The road is safe to cross.

Ryder, Marshall and Rocky are at the windmill.

"Let's get the electricity working for Chase's party," says Ryder, removing the broken blade.

"We can fix it with Zuma's old surfboard!" says Rocky. "Why lose it when you can reuse it!"

Marshall raises his ladder and Rocky climbs up. He attaches the surfboard to the windmill. Soon the wind picks up and it starts to turn!

"We did it!" shout Ryder, Marshall and Rocky.

Back at the Pet Parlour, the pups are playing in the dark when the lights come back on.

"Ryder and the PAW Patrol did it!" says Katie.

"But it's too late to bake a birthday cake," says Skye.

"I have an idea," says Katie.

On Main Street, the traffic lights come back on.

"Ryder and the PAW Patrol did it!" says Chase. "All right, everyone, it's safe to cross."

"Thanks, Chase!" say the people on Main Street.

Just then, Ryder calls. "Chase. Change of plans. We need you at Katie's."

"On my way!" barks Chase.

Next, Ryder calls Skye. "Chase is on his way and so are we!" he tells her.

"Great!" says Skye. "The surprise is all ready."

When Chase arrives at Katie's Pet Parlour, all the lights are off.

"Hello, anybody home?" he calls.

"SURPRISE!" everyone shouts, jumping out from behind the counter. "Happy Birthday, Chase!"

"You turned on the lights *and* made a party for me?" says Chase.

"Whenever it's your birthday, just yelp for help!" laughs Ryder.

"We couldn't make you a real cake, so I hope you like your dog biscuit cake," says Katie.

"It's Chase's birthday," says Ryder, "but you've *all* been really good pups. Dig in!"

Chase blows out the candles and everyone cheers, then the pups eat cake!